Animal Testing

Gail Terp

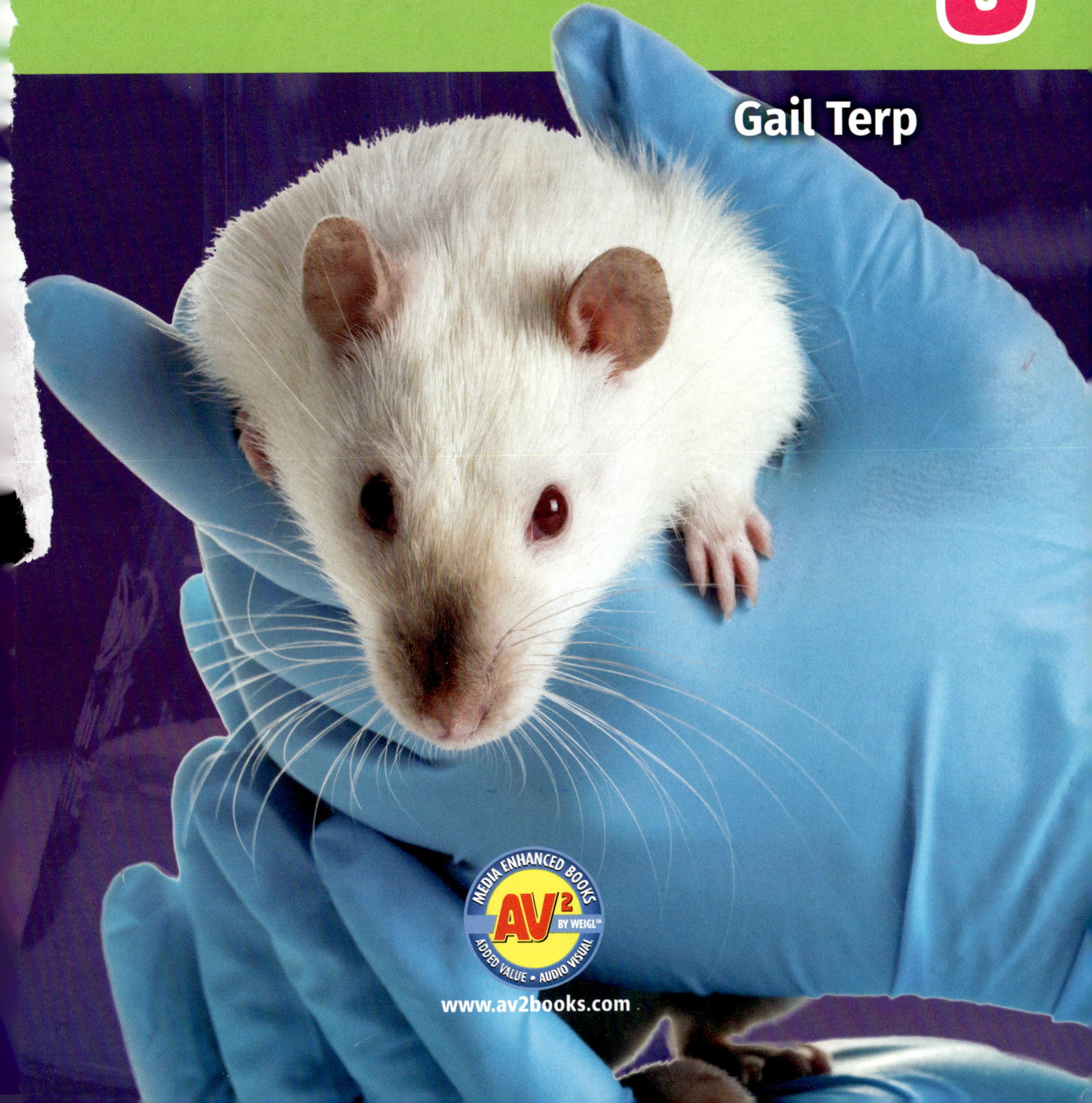

AV² provides enriched content that supplements and complements this book. Weigl's AV² books strive to create inspired learning and engage young minds in a total learning experience.

Your AV² Media Enhanced books come alive with...

 **Audio** Listen to sections of the book read aloud.

 **Key Words** Study vocabulary, and complete a matching word activity.

Go to www.av2books.com, and enter this book's unique code.

 **Video** Watch informative video clips.

 **Quizzes** Test your knowledge.

BOOK CODE

AVV97593

 **Embedded Weblinks** Gain additional information for research.

 **Slide Show** View images and captions, and prepare a presentation.

AV² by Weigl brings you media enhanced books that support active learning.

 **Try This!** Complete activities and hands-on experiments.

... and much, much more!

Published by AV² by Weigl
350 5th Avenue, 59th Floor New York, NY 10118
Website: www.av2books.com

Copyright © 2020 AV² by Weigl
All rights reserved. No part of this publication may be reproduced, stored in a retrieval system, or transmitted in any form or by any means, electronic, mechanical, photocopying, recording, or otherwise, without the prior written permission of the publisher.

Library of Congress Cataloging-in-Publication Data

Names: Terp, Gail, author.
Title: Animal testing / Gail Terp.
Other titles: Debate about animal testing
Description: New York, NY : AV² by Weigl, [2019] | Series: Debating the issues | Audience: Grade 7 to 8. | Includes index.
Identifiers: LCCN 2018053456 (print) | LCCN 2018054165 (ebook) | ISBN 9781489696274 (Multi User Ebook) | ISBN 9781489696281 (Single User Ebook) | ISBN 9781489696250 (hardcover : alk. paper) | ISBN 9781489696267 (softcover : alk. paper)
Subjects: LCSH: Animal experimentation--Moral and ethical aspects--Juvenile literature.
Classification: LCC HV4915 (ebook) | LCC HV4915 .T47 2019 (print) | DDC 179/.4--dc23
LC record available at https://lccn.loc.gov/2018053456

Printed in the United States of America in Brainerd, Minnesota
1 2 3 4 5 6 7 8 9 0   22 21 20 19 18

122018
112318

First published by North Star in 2018

Project Coordinator: John Willis   Designer: Ana María Vidal

Every reasonable effort has been made to trace ownership and to obtain permission to reprint copyright material. The publishers would be pleased to have any errors or omissions brought to their attention so that they may be corrected in subsequent printings.

Weigl acknowledges Getty Images, iStock, Shutterstock, and Alamy as its primary image suppliers for this title.

Animal Testing

Contents

Introduction to Animal Testing ... 4
Timeline 7

PROS
Animal Testing Leads to Medical Breakthroughs 8
Animal Testing is Accurate and Precise 14
Laws Protect Research Animals 20

CONS
Animal Testing Causes Animals to Suffer 26
Animal Testing Does Not Predict Human Reactions 32
Alternative Methods Provide Better Results 38

Pros and Cons Summary 43
Animal Testing Map 44
Quiz 46
Key Words/Index 47
Log on to www.av2books.com 48

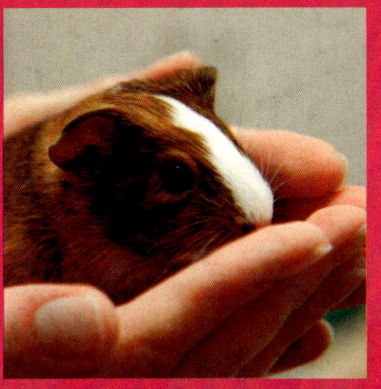

Studying animals such as mice helps researchers discover ways to treat and prevent diseases.

4 | Debating the Issues

Introduction to Animal Testing

Doctors and veterinarians strive to improve the health of their patients. They work to prevent and cure illness. Many illnesses cause exhaustion and severe pain. These **symptoms** can make it difficult to work or feel pleasure. Treating illness is often expensive. But if left untreated, illnesses may cause additional suffering or even death. To learn of the best treatments, doctors often turn to medical research.

One way that scientists research illness is by using animals. Animals make good research subjects because they are so similar to humans. Rats, mice, fish, and birds make up the largest research group. These animals are used for 90 to 95 percent of the animal research in the United States. But research labs use many types of animals. They use cats, dogs, rabbits, guinea pigs, and hamsters. Labs also use farm animals such as sheep and pigs. Some labs use primates such as monkeys and chimpanzees.

Many medical breakthroughs have occurred because of animal testing. But not everyone agrees that animals should be used for testing. The methods used in the tests can harm the animals. In some cases, the tests do not provide reliable information. For these reasons, opponents of animal testing believe that medical researchers should use other methods instead. The debate about this complicated issue will likely continue for many years to come.

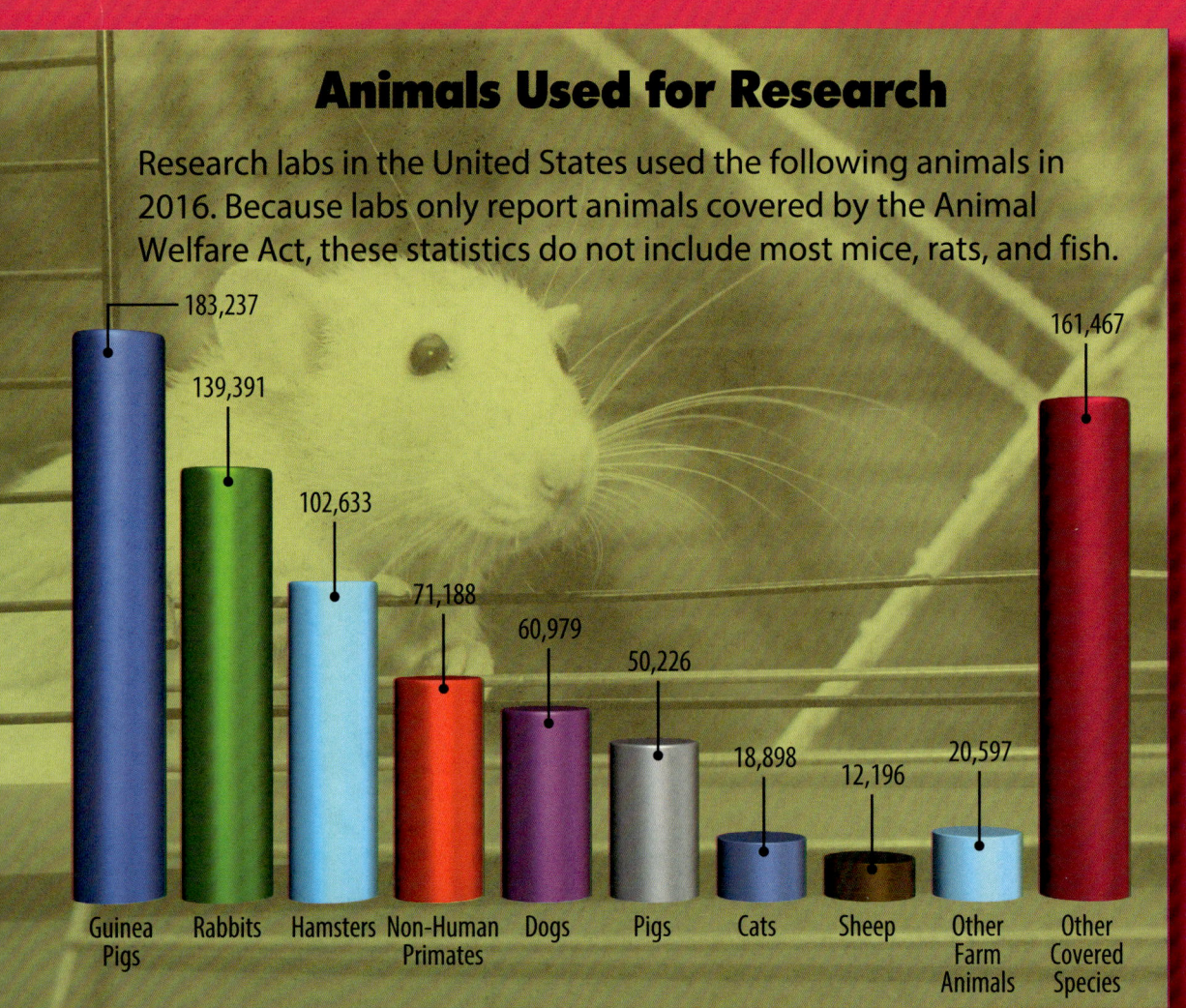

Animals Used for Research

Research labs in the United States used the following animals in 2016. Because labs only report animals covered by the Animal Welfare Act, these statistics do not include most mice, rats, and fish.

Guinea Pigs	183,237
Rabbits	139,391
Hamsters	102,633
Non-Human Primates	71,188
Dogs	60,979
Pigs	50,226
Cats	18,898
Sheep	12,196
Other Farm Animals	20,597
Other Covered Species	161,467

Timeline

1904 — Russian physiologist Ivan Petrovich Pavlov is awarded the Nobel Prize in Physiology or Medicine for his work using animals to understand digestion.

1938 — The United States Food, Drug and Cosmetic Act becomes law. This requires that cosmetics and drugs be tested to ensure their safety.

1959 — In their book, *The Principles of Humane Experimental Technique*, William Russell and Rex Burch create guidelines known as the Three Rs of animal testing.

1966 — The Animal Welfare Act becomes law, setting care requirements for animals. However, many common test animals are not included in the law.

2000 — The Interagency Coordination Committee on the Validation of Alternative Methods (ICCVAM) is established to research alternatives to animal testing.

2018 — California becomes the first U.S. state to ban cosmetics that are tested on animals. This law will take effect on January 1, 2020.

PRO

Research with animals helped scientists learn how to manage diabetes.

Animal Testing Leads to Medical Breakthroughs

Animal testing has led to many important medical discoveries. Diseases that once caused great suffering and even death can now be treated. For example, research with dogs in the 1920s helped scientists find a treatment for diabetes. When people have diabetes, their bodies cannot regulate **glucose**. In addition to causing fatigue, this disease can lead to kidney or nerve damage.

Animal testing helped researchers learn that diabetes affects an organ called the pancreas. In 1921, researchers did surgery to remove this organ from several dogs. After the surgery, the dogs developed diabetes. The researchers discovered that the pancreas produces a chemical called insulin. Insulin controls and adjusts the body's use of sugars and starches. When researchers gave the dogs injections of insulin, the dogs' diabetes improved.

Did You Know?

In the past decade, research with mice has led to surgery that improves vision in people who are blind.

10 | Debating the Issues

Today, pacemakers are about the same size as a large coin.

The researchers realized that diabetes occurs when the body does not produce enough insulin. In 1922, the first person received an insulin injection. This treatment was successful. Soon, insulin was used to help many people.

Research with animals also helped scientists understand heart disease. This serious disease can lead to heart attacks or death. But scientists have found several ways to treat heart disease. One treatment is a pacemaker. This device is placed inside a person's chest. It helps control the person's heartbeat. The first pacemakers were created in the 1950s based on research with dogs.

Heart **transplants** are another way to treat heart disease. Doctors performed the first human heart transplant in 1967. Research with dogs also helped make this important achievement possible.

Hypertension often leads to heart disease. Testing with rats or primates helps researchers find ways to treat this condition. Researchers in the 2000s found that baboons and humans can have the same kind of hypertension. Studying baboons may help researchers understand which **genes** cause this problem.

The cancer survival rate in the United States has doubled since the 1970s. This is largely due to animal research. Researchers use mice to learn about leukemia. In this form of cancer, the body forms too many white blood cells. Studying mice that have leukemia helps researchers create new drugs and treatments for the disease.

Animal testing may lead to new treatments for other diseases as well. For instance, Alzheimer's is a brain disease that causes memory loss. Scientists are studying animals to look for a cure. Current research with sea snails may reveal how and where brains store memories.

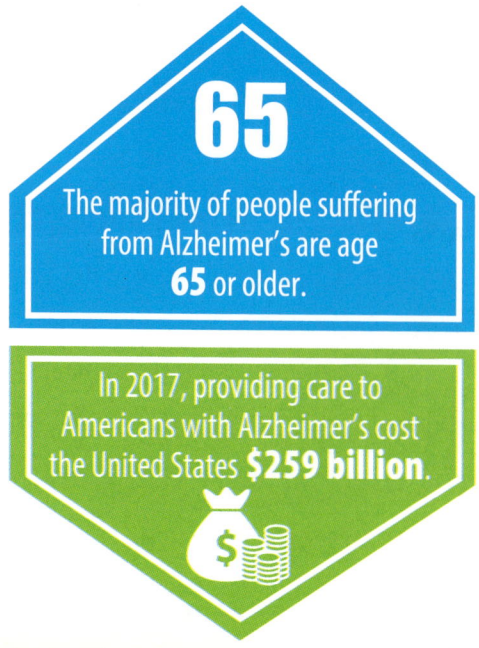

12 | Debating the Issues

Mice can be used to study heart disease, seizures, and the immune system.

Animal Testing | 13

PRO

14 | Debating the Issues

Animal Testing is Accurate and Precise

The genes of mammals, such as chimpanzees, are similar to human genes.

Some people believe that researchers should create computer models or study human body cells instead of using animal testing. But these methods do not provide enough information. The bodies of humans and animals are made up of many organs, blood vessels, and nerves. All parts of the body system must work together.

Ferrets are used in research about the heart, the brain, and the digestive system.

Each individual part is made up of cells. Each cell is more complicated than a computer program. In fact, these systems are too complex for computers to replicate. Studying body cells alone cannot show researchers how a disease or treatment affects the entire body.

Many animals have the same organs as humans. Their blood vessels and nerves are similar, too. Because their bodies are so similar, animals and humans often get the same diseases. Working with animals helps researchers understand how these diseases affect humans.

For example, the flu is an illness that causes a fever, weakness, and breathing problems in humans. The virus that causes the flu changes frequently. Therefore, scientists must develop new flu vaccines every year. Ferrets can also get the flu. They suffer from the same symptoms as humans. Studying ferrets that have the flu has helped scientists test and develop new flu vaccines. These vaccines can help prevent humans from getting sick.

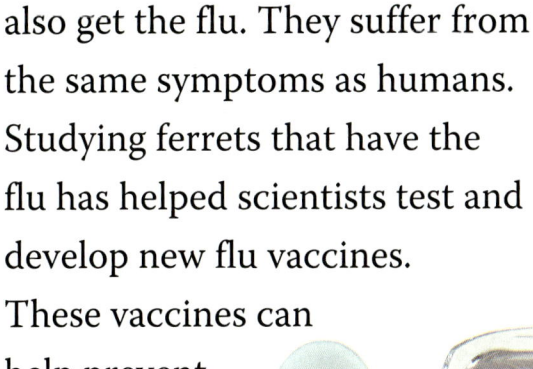

Each year, vaccines prevent between 2 and 3 million deaths worldwide.

Animal Testing | 17

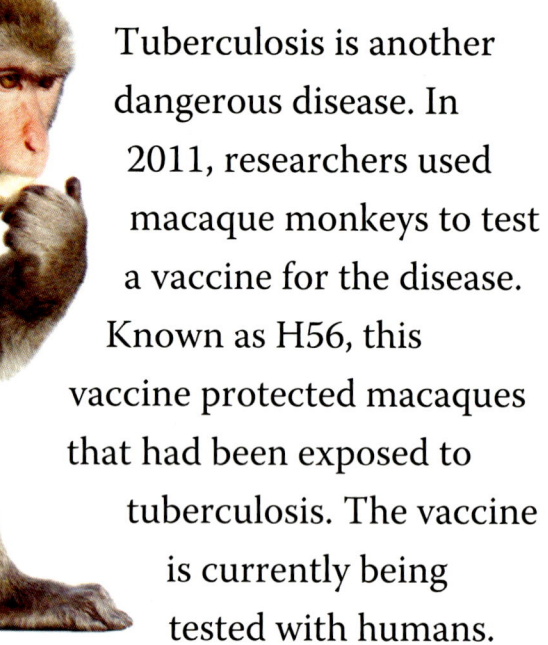

Tuberculosis is another dangerous disease. In 2011, researchers used macaque monkeys to test a vaccine for the disease. Known as H56, this vaccine protected macaques that had been exposed to tuberculosis. The vaccine is currently being tested with humans.

About one third of monkeys in Asia are affected by tuberculosis. This is one of the reasons why they were used to test H56.

Transgenic Animals

Researchers alter the genes of some lab animals. One or more genes are transferred to the animal from another species. These animals, often mice, are called transgenic animals. They often have their genes changed to model a human disease. Work with transgenic mice has led to new drugs and treatments. These include ways to treat heart disease, diabetes, and cancer.

Even the genes of animals and humans are similar. Genes control much of how a living being looks and acts. Therefore, testing the reactions of animals is a good way to predict how humans might react. For example, mice have more than 95 percent of the same genes as humans. Mice are often used in cancer drug research. In a 2017 study, researchers gave a drug called *cabozantinib* to mice that had cancer. The drug caused their cancer to disappear. It is now being tested with humans.

Researchers can control the conditions in the labs where they do animal testing. Carefully monitoring the lab's temperature and light, as well as the animals' diet and health, helps researchers make sure their results will be as accurate as possible.

Rats and mice make up 95 percent of all lab animals.

Animal Testing | 19

Research labs must make sure their animals have adequate socialization.

Laws Protect Research Animals

Animal Testing | 21

Comfortable housing for rodents includes access to water and places to hide.

In the United States, federal and state laws protect the animals that are used for research. These laws help ensure the animals are properly cared for. According to the laws, lab animals must have clean housing and access to fresh air. Animals must also receive enough food and water. For example, the laws require labs to feed cats and dogs at least once a day. Cats and dogs must have access to water at least two times each day. The laws also give specific instructions for each type of animal. Cats must have access to clean litter. Dogs must have a place to exercise. Primates and marine mammals also have their own sets of rules.

Research labs must provide proper medical care for the animals. They are required to have a veterinarian who can **diagnose** and treat any diseases or injuries. In addition, lab staff must monitor the animals' health. They are required to observe each animal every day.

Each research lab also has a committee that inspects all its work with animals. This committee makes sure research labs follow the laws. Other inspectors examine each lab at least once a year. They check how the lab cares for, treats, and uses its animals. They also make sure the animals feel little or no pain and distress.

Laboratory animal veterinarians take care of the animals used in research labs.

Animal Testing | 23

Additional guidelines for research labs were created in the 1950s. Known as the Three Rs, these guidelines stand for *replacement*, *reduction*, and *refinement*.

Replacement guidelines urge researchers to use alternate methods whenever possible. For example, suppose a computer model of the heart can provide the same results as animal testing. The replacement guidelines ask researchers to use the model instead. Replacement guidelines also recommend using the simplest animal possible. For instance, mice are considered simpler than dogs. Therefore, researchers would try to use mice for testing instead of dogs.

In research labs, tools such as computer programs are known as "absolute replacements" because no animal is used.

The reduction guidelines ask labs to use fewer animals when they conduct tests. Researchers design their tests to use the smallest possible number of animals. They also collect as much information as they can from each set of animals instead of running many tests.

The refinement guidelines aim to improve conditions for lab animals. This applies to all parts of the animals' care, not only the tests. Researchers make sure animals have adequate living situations. For example, mice are less stressed when they have comfortable and interesting housing.

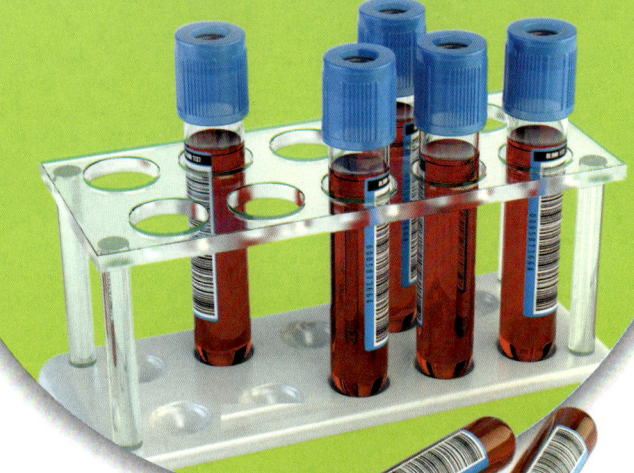

Did You Know?
Animals that are less stressed tend to produce more accurate test results.

Using simpler animals instead of more complex ones is an example of "relative replacement."

Animal Testing | 25

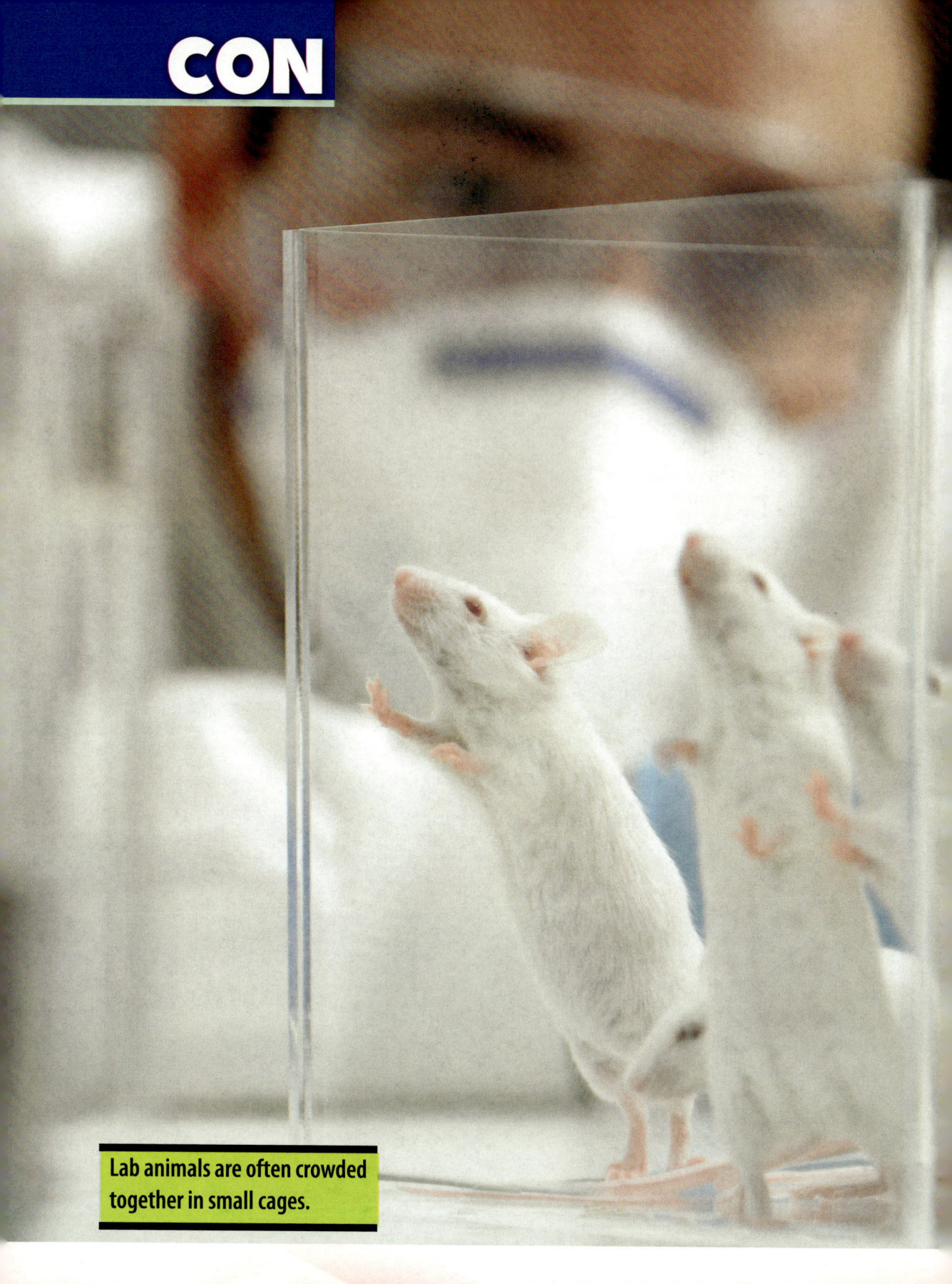

Lab animals are often crowded together in small cages.

Animal Testing Causes Animals to Suffer

Unfortunately, the animal protection system has many problems. Most animal protection laws do not include rats, mice, fish, and birds. These animals make up more than 90 percent of animals tested.

In addition, research labs usually choose the people who are part of their supervising group. As a result, group members may do what is best for the lab instead of what is best for the animals. Other lab inspectors must inspect large numbers of animals and test **procedures**. These inspectors may only visit most labs only once per year. For these reasons, it can be easy for them to miss many problems.

On March 11, 2013, the European Union banned the use of animals to test cosmetic products.

28 | Debating the Issues

Groups such as Cruelty Free International investigate animal research labs. These groups look at how the labs care for their animals and how researchers conduct their experiments. They have found many examples of animal suffering.

Research animals often live in poor conditions. In one lab, rabbit cages had no bedding to cover their floors. The cages hurt the rabbits' feet. Some rabbits died from their injuries. Other animals live in crowded cages and have little room to move. In other cases, they may be forced to live alone.

In addition, animals may be harmed during experiments. For instance, one lab used hundreds of monkeys for brain research. The monkeys spent their entire lives in cages. Researchers gave them brain damage as part of the study.

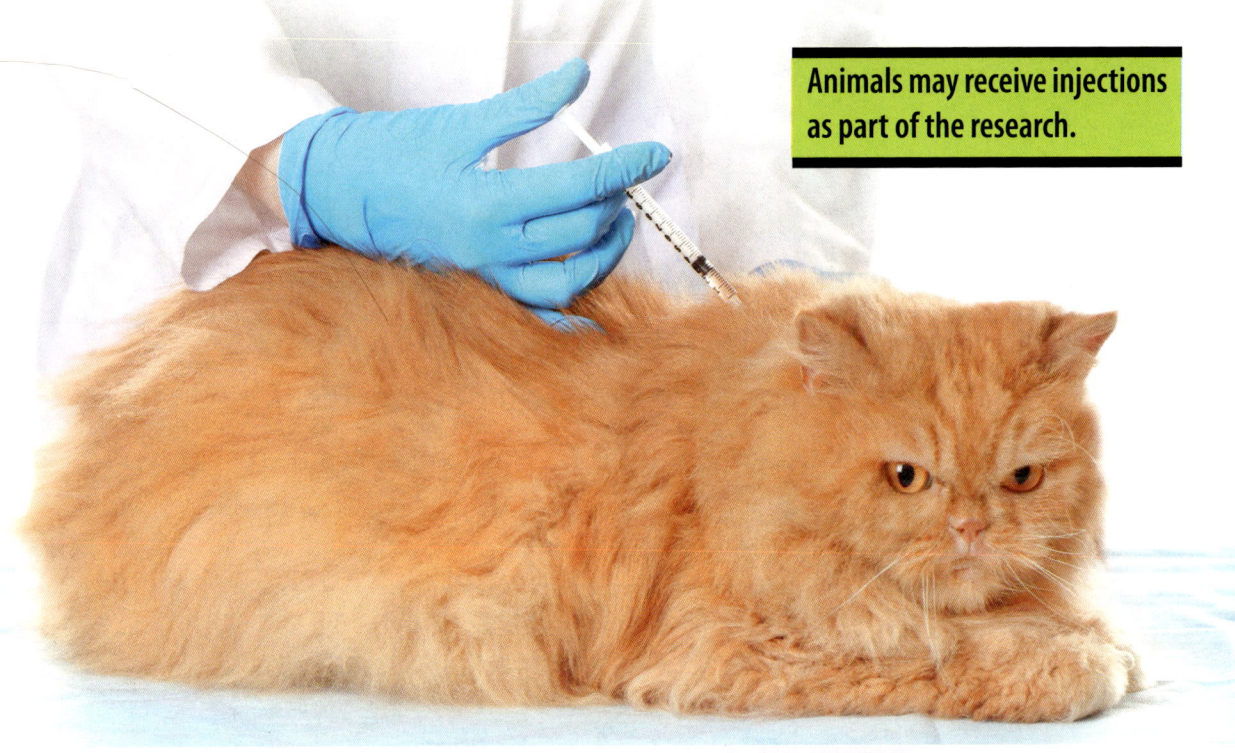

Animals may receive injections as part of the research.

Animal Testing | 29

Other tests may require animals to go without food or water. Sometimes animals receive food as a reward for learning new tasks. Before these tests, researchers may withhold the animals' food. They do so with the hope that hunger will motivate the animals to learn the tasks.

Researchers may also restrain the animals. An animal may be unable to move part or all of its body during the test. This can last for hours, days, or months. For example, monkeys were not given water for 22 hours as part of one research project. Then each monkey was placed in a restraining chair for an hour. Researchers gave the monkey vision tasks. They gave the monkey only one drop of water each time it performed a task.

In other tests, researchers give animals drugs or chemicals and observe how they respond. These tests are often painful. They may even be fatal. For instance, a test known as LD50 is used to determine how toxic a chemical is. In this test, animals are force-fed the chemical until half of them die. Researchers may even give animals diseases to test if new treatments are effective.

In 2013, the National Institutes of Health (NIH) in the United States announced that it would phase out research using chimpanzees.

30 | Debating the Issues

Animal Suffering

Animals are affected in many ways by different kinds of tests. Some of these tests may result in permanent injury or death.

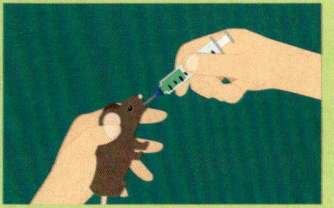

Toxicity
Animals breathe, ingest, or are injected with a chemical, and researchers study how different amounts of the chemical affect the animal. This test often results in the death of the animals.

Eye Irritation
Animals have chemicals dropped into their eyes, and researchers study any irritation or injury that results. This test often results in redness, bleeding, or blindness.

Skin Irritation
Animals are shaved and have a chemical placed on their skin, and researchers study how it damages the animals' skin. This test often results in painful scabs, bleeding, or sores.

Reproductive Toxicity
Animals are given chemicals such as pesticides to see how these chemicals affect their ability to reproduce. This test often results in illness or death.

Developmental Toxicity
Animal embryos are examined to determine if or how the chemical affected their development. This test requires the death of both the pregnant animal and the embryos.

Animal Testing

CON

The drug penicillin causes vomiting in guinea pigs, but it is safe for humans to use.

Animal Testing Does Not Predict Human Reactions

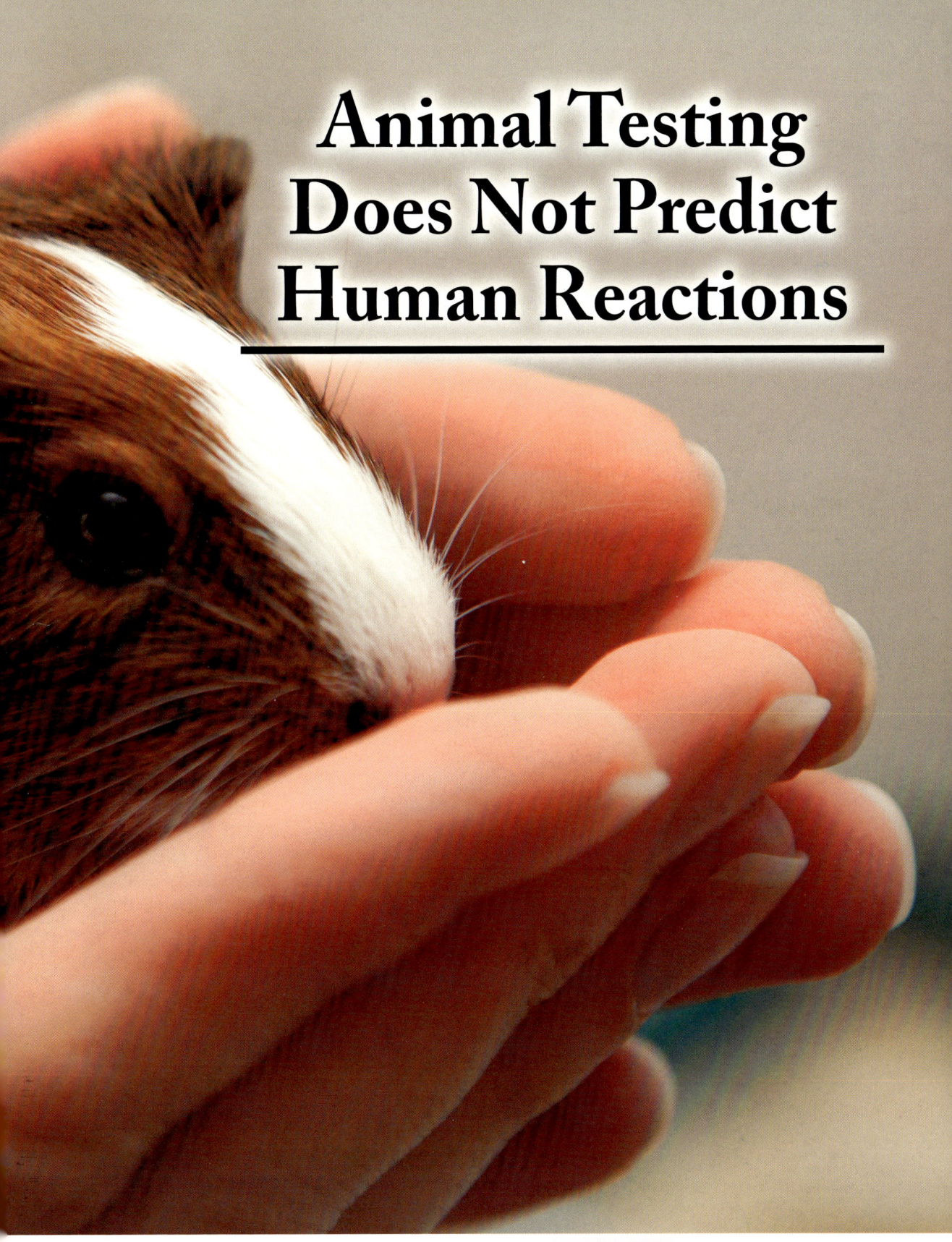

For years, researchers have used animals to test chemicals and medications. They assume that because animals are similar to humans, the results of the tests can predict how humans will react. However, each species' body is different. An animal will not respond to a treatment or drug the same way that a person would. As a result, testing drugs on animals can create results that do not apply to humans.

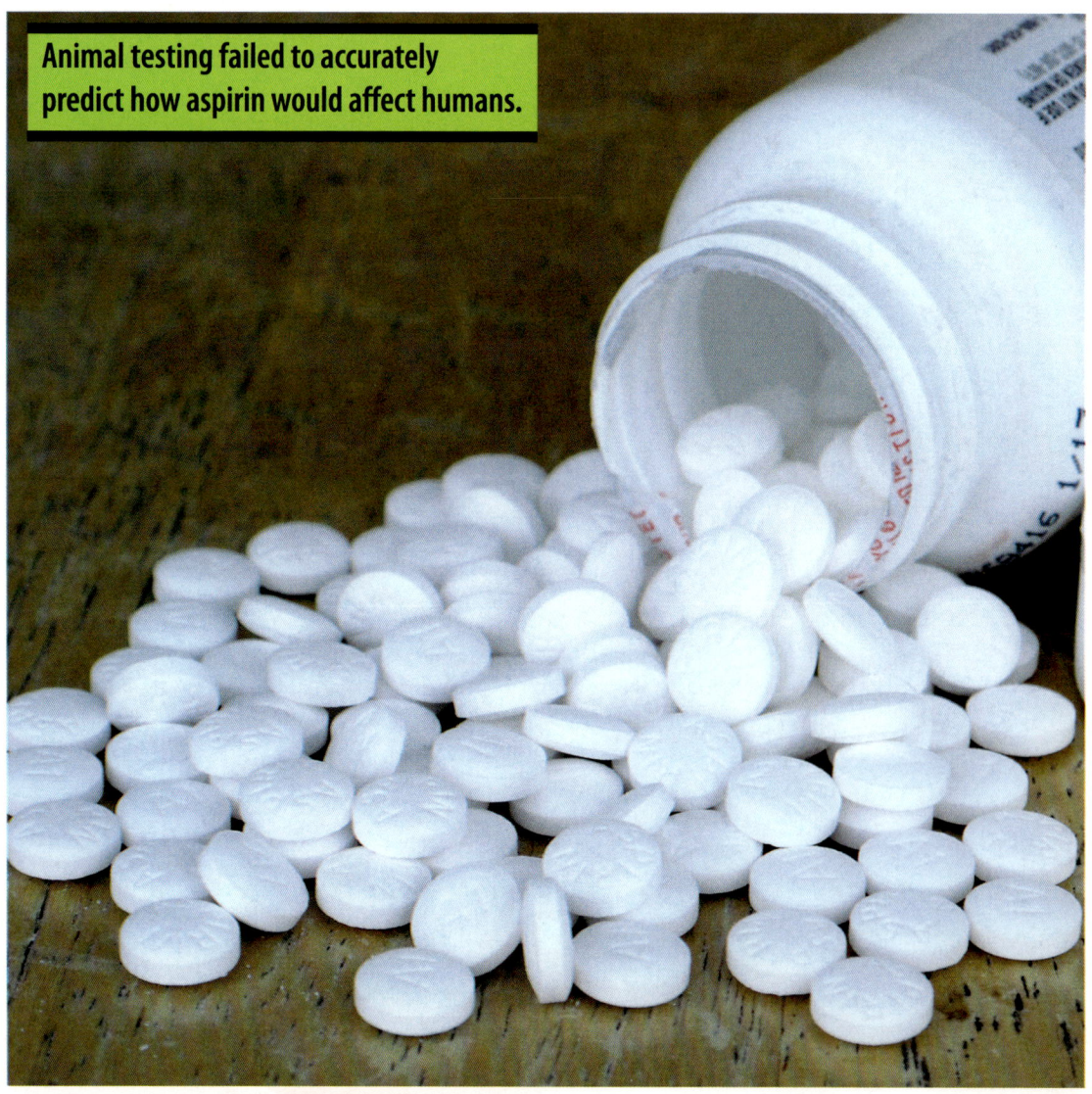

Animal testing failed to accurately predict how aspirin would affect humans.

In addition, the animals live in research labs. The lab environment is highly controlled. This is much different from the regular world. Everyday life involves many more factors that can vary or change. Tests in a lab environment do not account for these factors. As a result, the tests cannot reliably predict what will work for people.

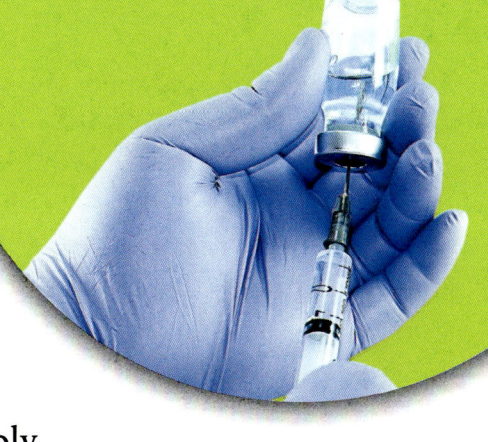

Did You Know?

More than 80 vaccines for HIV worked when tested on chimpanzees but are not safe or effective for humans.

In fact, some drugs that did not work when tested on animals have been quite helpful for humans. For example, aspirin is a drug that can decrease pain, lower fevers, and reduce **inflammation**. But this valuable medicine failed terribly when researchers tested it on animals. Aspirin caused problems for mice, rats, dogs, and cats. When it was tested with humans, however, it proved to be safe.

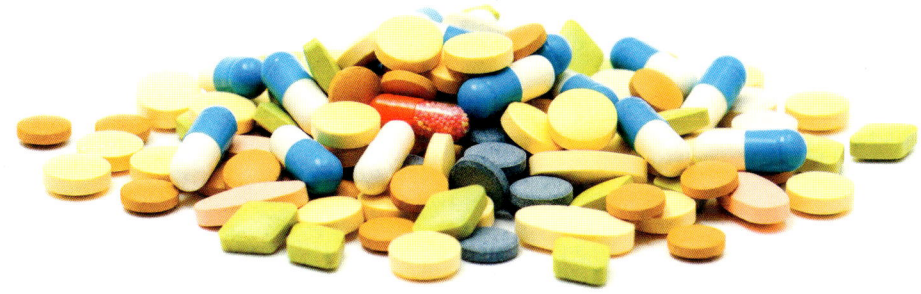

Many drugs in use today failed when they were tested on animals. Some of these drugs treat heart conditions or stomach problems. Others reduce pain. Some even fight infection or cancer. The differences between humans and animals may cause researchers to overlook drugs that could be helpful.

The opposite is also true. Drugs that pass animal tests can be harmful to humans. Some of these medicines can cause serious illnesses or heart problems. In some cases, drugs that pass animal testing can be fatal to humans.

For example, researchers tested a painkiller called Vioxx on several species of animals. The animals did not show any symptoms, so the drug was approved in 1999. But Vioxx caused serious illness and death in humans. The company that created Vioxx stopped selling the drug in 2004. By then, approximately 88,000 people in the United States had suffered from heart attacks after taking the drug. More than 35,000 of these people died.

Taking Vioxx doubled a person's risk of getting a heart attack or stroke.

The African green monkey, one animal used to test Vioxx, is often used for research about diseases and vaccines.

African green monkeys were introduced to the **Caribbean** in the 1600s.

Cells from one African green monkey's **kidney** helped scientists develop vaccines for **polio** and **smallpox**.

Animal Testing | 37

CON

Both humans and animals can be safely scanned.

38 | Debating the Issues

Alternative Methods Provide Better Results

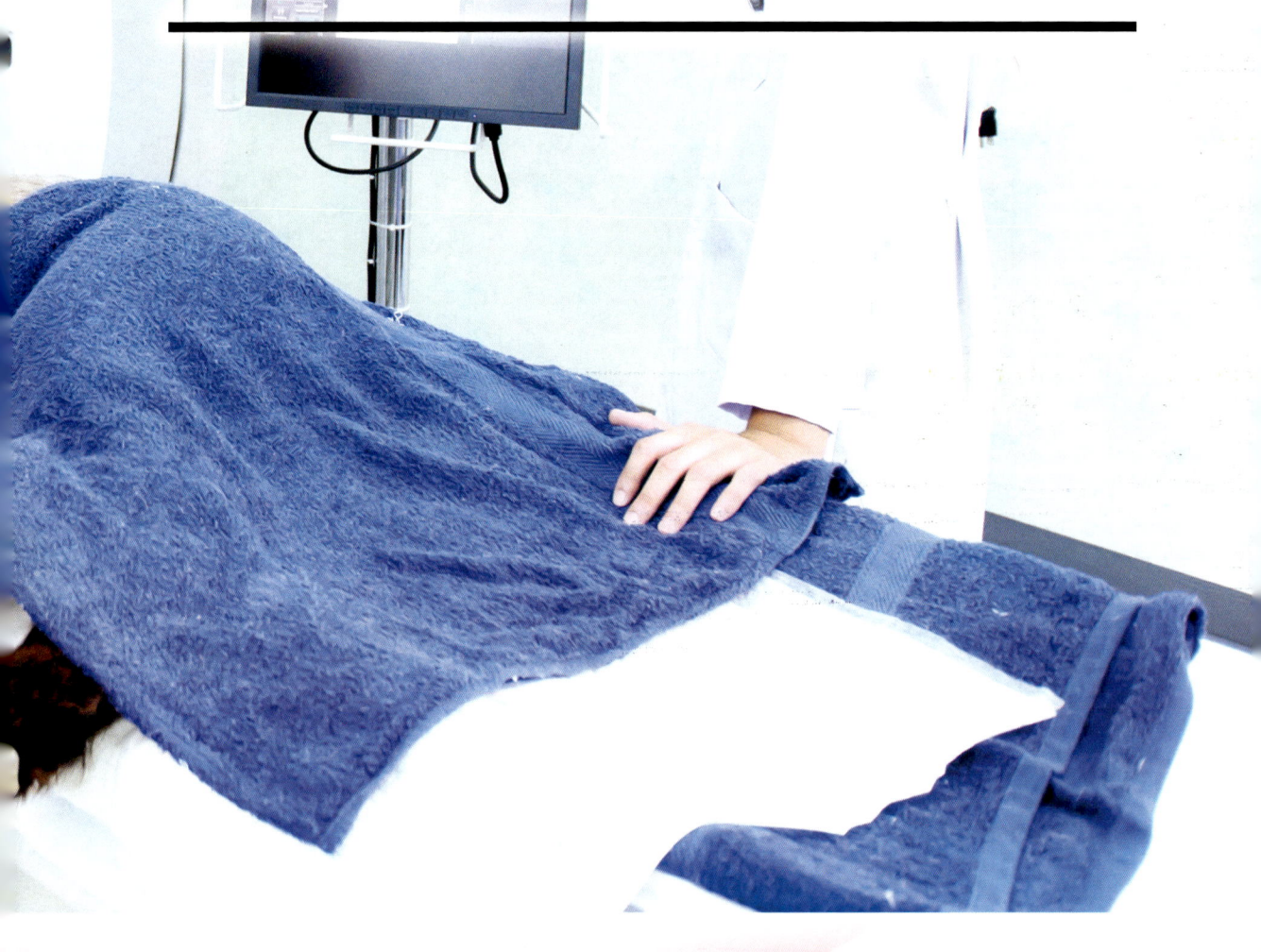

Animal Testing | 39

Today, researchers have many options for alternatives to animal testing. For instance, **MRI scans** can capture images of an animal's internal organs. Unlike surgery, the scans are painless. Plus, researchers can scan one animal multiple times instead of performing surgery on several animals. This reduces the number of animals needed for testing. MRI scans can even be used to study human organs and diseases.

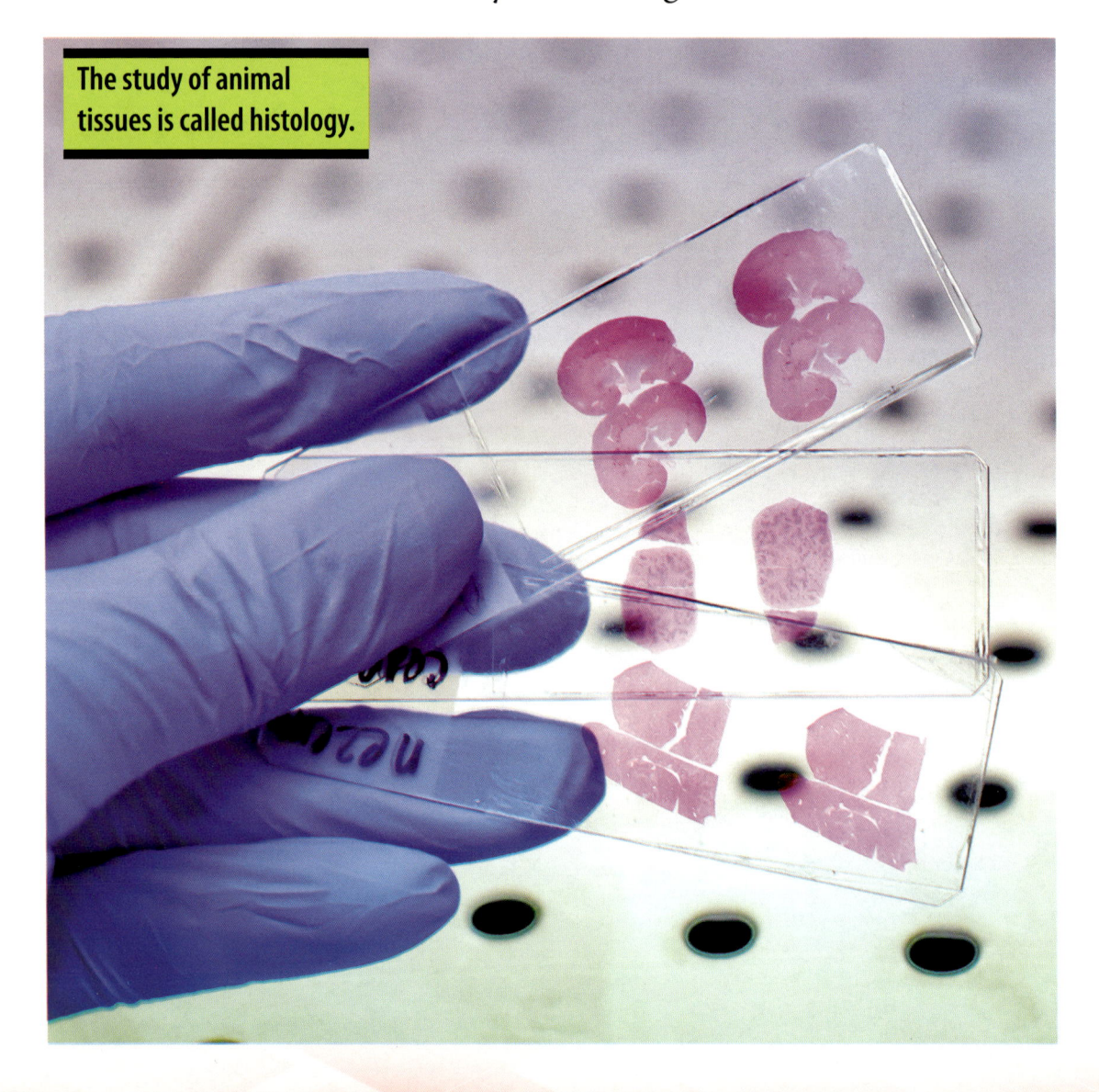

The study of animal tissues is called histology.

Debating the Issues

Other alternative methods can completely replace animal tests. The cell culture method allows researchers to study human cells instead of using animals. In this method, researchers collect samples of human cells or tissues. Then they grow the cells in test tubes in a research lab. Researchers study the cells as they grow to understand how the cells function. They can even use the cells to create models of diseases. This process allows researchers to test how the diseases would respond to different drugs or chemicals.

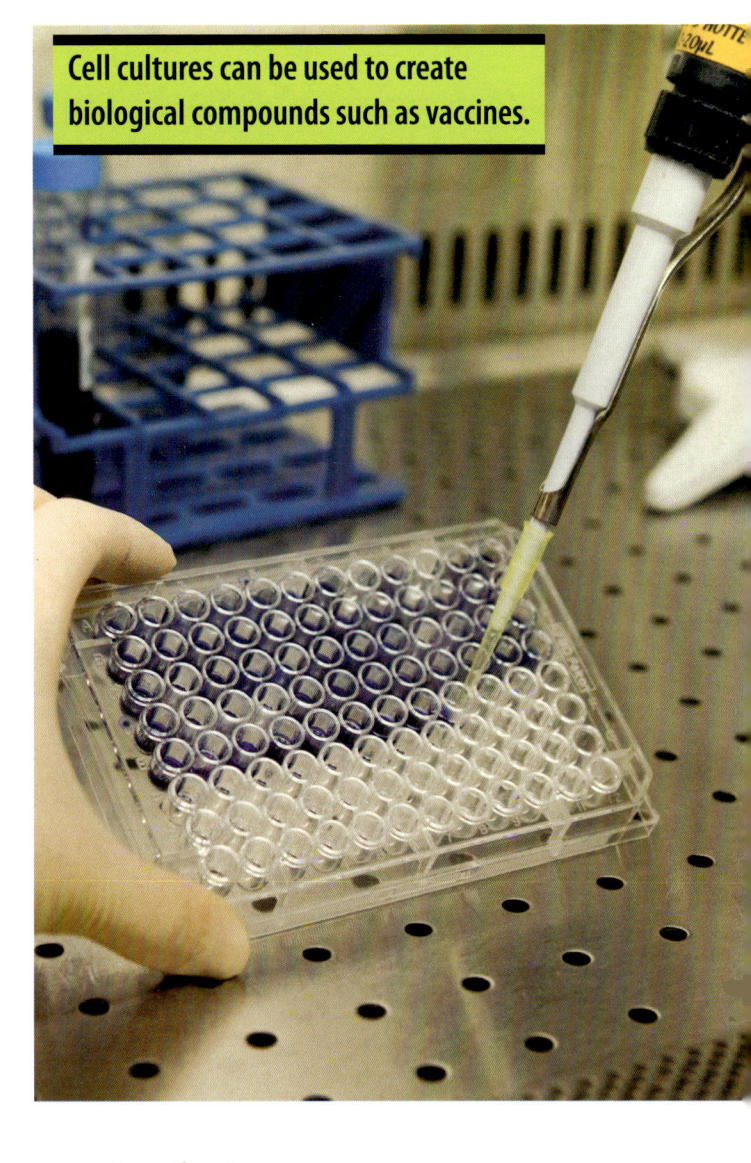

Cell cultures can be used to create biological compounds such as vaccines.

Researchers can also use computer **simulation** programs. The programs create models of human body systems and diseases. Researchers use the models to predict how new drugs will work in humans. For example, some computer programs test cancer drugs. The programs help predict how a patient's tumor will respond to a drug. This process helps doctors choose the best treatment for the patient.

Animal Testing | 41

Microdosing uses human volunteers to test new drugs. Volunteers receive tiny doses of the drug that are too small to cause a bad reaction. A highly sensitive device follows the path the drug takes through the body. It shows how the drug affects the body.

These alternative tests produce results without harming animals. They are often faster and less expensive than animal testing, too. Fewer people are needed to run the tests, and researchers do not need to house or care for animals.

Many alternative methods are based on human cells and organs. Because these methods work with models of the human body instead of animal bodies, the results tend to be more reliable. These methods provide an ethical and effective alternative to animal testing.

Organs-on-Chips

Organs-on-chips are one alternative to animal testing. To create them, researchers remove living cells from a human organ. They place the cells inside a small piece of clear plastic, or microchip. Studying the microchips helps researchers learn about the human body. For example, the lung-on-a-chip imitates the tiny air sacs in a lung. Researchers have also developed chips that mimic kidneys, skin, and intestines.

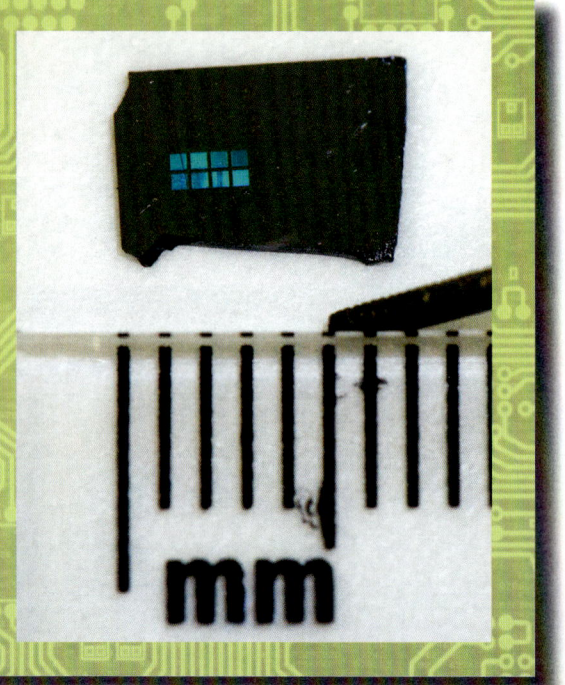

Pros and Cons Summary

PROS

- Animal testing helps researchers learn how to treat and prevent deadly diseases.
- Animal testing helps researchers understand how organs and body systems work.
- Using animals with similar genes to humans produces accurate test results.
- Animal testing allows researchers to control the testing environment.
- Animal testing laws make sure that the animals in research labs are treated well.
- Research guidelines ensure that testing is done only when necessary.

CONS

- Animal protection laws do not apply to 90 percent of animals used in research labs.
- Animal protection laws are often not enforced well, so many animals have poor living conditions.
- Many research procedures cause animals pain and suffering.
- Animal testing cannot reliably predict how humans will react to drugs or chemicals.
- Drugs that are safe for animals may still be dangerous to humans.
- Several alternative testing methods produce more accurate results and can be less expensive.

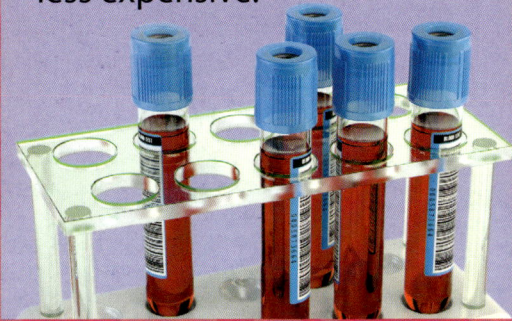

Animal Testing Map

Pacific Ocean

North America

South America

Atlantic Ocean

Today, animal testing takes place all around the world. However, many companies, organizations, and governments are attempting to switch over to other testing methods that are just as accurate but do not require living subjects.

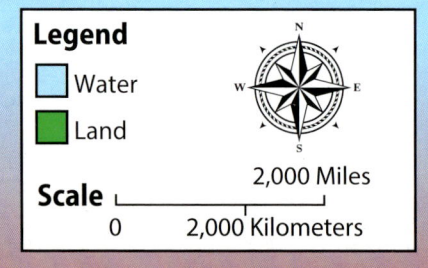

United States
In 2000, an area of land in Keithville, Louisiana, was set aside as a home for retired laboratory chimpanzees. Today, more than 200 chimpanzees live in Chimp Haven.

Legend
- Water
- Land

Scale 0 — 2,000 Miles / 2,000 Kilometers

Debating the Issues

Great Britain
Scottish bacteriologist Alexander Fleming discovered penicillin at St. Mary's Hospital, London, in 1928. After it was tested on mice in 1940, it quickly entered mass production.

India
In 2016, the Ministry of Health and Family Welfare, headquartered in New Delhi, passed a ban on animal testing for drugs that have already been tested in Organisation for Economic Co-operation and Development (OECD) countries.

Belgium
In 2013, the European Commission, headquartered in Brussels, banned animal testing in cosmetic items. This ban applies to all European Union members.

Animal Testing | 45

Quiz

1 Which animals are not included in most animal protection laws?

2 Why do humans and other animals often get the same diseases?

3 What was the first U.S. state to ban cosmetics tested on animals?

4 Which painkiller was approved in 1999 but withdrawn because it could cause serious injury or death in humans?

5 What is the study of animal tissues called?

6 How has the cancer survival rate in the United States changed since 1970?

7 What are the Three Rs of animal testing?

8 When were the first pacemakers created?

ANSWERS: 1. Rats, mice, fish, and birds **2.** Because their bodies are relatively similar **3.** California **4.** Vioxx **5.** Histology **6.** It has doubled **7.** Replacement, reduction, and refinement **8.** The 1950s

46 | Debating the Issues

Key Words

diagnose: to determine the disease that a person or animal has

genes: tiny parts of cells that tell the cells how to perform certain functions or cause the body to develop certain traits

glucose: a sugar found in plants that is converted to energy by the body

hypertension: an unhealthy level of high blood pressure

inflammation: heat, redness, and swelling that are part of the body's response to disease

MRI scans: procedures that use radio waves and a strong magnet to produce detailed images of the inside of the body

procedures: established ways or orders of doing something

simulation: something that is made to look or feel like something else

symptoms: signs of an illness or disease

transplants: surgeries in which an organ or other body part is removed from one person or animal and placed into the body of another person or animal

Index

cancer 12, 18, 19, 36, 41, 46
cell culture 41
cells 12, 16, 17, 37, 41, 42
chimpanzees 5, 15, 30, 35, 44
computer simulation 41

diabetes 8, 10, 11, 18
dogs 5, 6, 10, 11, 22, 24, 35
drug 7, 12, 18, 19, 30, 32, 34, 35, 36, 41, 42, 43, 45

genes 12, 15, 18, 19, 43

heart disease 11, 12, 13, 18, 36

injections 10, 11, 29

law 7, 21, 22, 23, 28, 43, 46

mice 4, 5, 6, 10, 12, 13, 18, 19, 24, 25, 28, 35, 45, 46
microdosing 42
MRI scans 40

organ 10, 16, 17, 40, 42, 43
organs-on-chips 42

pain 5, 23, 30, 31, 35, 36, 40, 43, 46

primates 5, 6, 12, 22

suffering 5, 10, 12, 17, 27, 29, 31, 43
surgery 10, 40

Three Rs 7, 24, 25, 46
toxic 30, 31
transgenic animals 18
transplants 11

vaccines 17, 18, 35, 37, 41
Vioxx 36, 37, 46

Animal Testing | 47

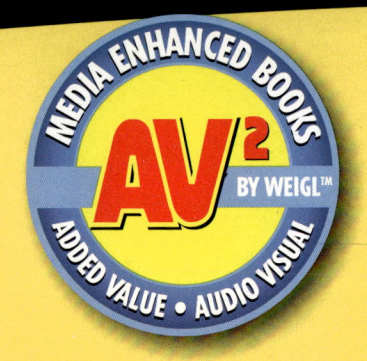

Log on to www.av2books.com

AV² by Weigl brings you media enhanced books that support active learning. Go to www.av2books.com, and enter the special code found on page 2 of this book. You will gain access to enriched and enhanced content that supplements and complements this book. Content includes video, audio, weblinks, quizzes, a slide show, and activities.

AV² Online Navigation

Book Pages
AV² pages directly correspond to pages in the book.

Key Words
Study vocabulary, and complete a matching word activity.

Quizzes
Test your knowledge.

Slide Show
View images and captions, and prepare a presentation.

Audio
Listen to sections of the book read aloud.

Video
Watch informative video clips.

Embedded Weblinks
Gain additional information for research.

Try This!
Complete activities and hands-on experiments.

AV² was built to bridge the gap between print and digital. We encourage you to tell us what you like and what you want to see in the future.

Sign up to be an AV² Ambassador at www.av2books.com/ambassador.

Due to the dynamic nature of the Internet, some of the URLs and activities provided as part of AV² by Weigl may have changed or ceased to exist. AV² by Weigl accepts no responsibility for any such changes. All media enhanced books are regularly monitored to update addresses and sites in a timely manner. Contact AV² by Weigl at 1-866-649-3445 or av2books@weigl.com with any questions, comments, or feedback.